PEDRO AND THE
SHARK

by Fran Manushkin

illustrated by
Tammie Lyon

SCHOLASTIC INC.

ISBN 978-1-338-28110-1

18 17 16 9 8 7 6 5 4 3 2 1   22 23 24 25

Printed in the U.S.A.   40

First Scholastic printing, January 2018

Designer: Tracy McCabe
Design Elements: Shutterstock

Table of Contents

Chapter 1
Something Fishy

Pedro told his dad, "I'm doing something fishy today."

"You are?" asked his dad.

"Yes!" Pedro smiled. "I'm going to the aquarium."

His dad laughed. "That *is* fishy!"

"I've saved some money,"
said Pedro. "I'm bringing back
a souvenir."

"Great!" said his dad. "I
can't wait to see it."

At the aquarium, Miss Winkle told the class, "Be sure to stay together."

"That's easy," said Pedro. "We can pretend we are minnows. They always stick together."

"It's cool in here," said

Katie. "And dark."

"Yes," added JoJo. "It's a

little spooky."

"Here comes something crabby!" said Pedro.

"Is it my baby brother?" joked Barry.

"Very funny!" said Miss Winkle. "It's a hermit crab."

"I love the starfish," said
Katie. "They look dreamy."
"But the jellyfish looks
lonely," said JoJo. "Maybe
he's looking for a peanut
butter fish."

"I'd love to take a ride on
the seahorse," said Pedro. "But
I would need to be smaller."

"Yes," said Katie. "And
don't forget your snorkel!"

Roddy ran ahead. "YAY!" he yelled. "Here come the sharks! *Duck!*"

"Yikes!" said Pedro. "Those teeth look sharp. I don't want to ride on *him*."

"You know," said Pedro,

"all this water is making me

thirsty."

He walked away to find a

water fountain.

Chapter 2
Alone with the Shark

When Pedro finished

drinking, he looked for his

class. They were gone.

Pedro was alone — with

the shark!

"See you later!" Pedro yelled. "I have to find my class."

"Here they are!" He smiled. "I see JoJo!"

No! It wasn't her.

"I bet my class is around this corner," said Pedro.

The room was dark and filled with whales.

"Yay!" yelled Pedro.

"Here's my class."

No! It *wasn't*!

Pedro ran

this way and

that way, but

he kept coming

back to the shark.

Pedro looked at the shark, who was swimming in circles.

"Ha!" Pedro smiled. "That's why I can't find my class! I've been going in circles. Thanks for the clue."

Chapter 3
Make Like a Turtle

Pedro tried a new direction.

He passed a sea turtle. She moved slowly, looking calm and wise.

"I'll try that," said Pedro.

Pedro took a deep breath.

He walked slowly. "I'll turn

left this time, then right."

Success! Pedro found his

class.

"Here you are!" said Miss Winkle. "We were going to start searching."

"I found you first," Pedro said proudly.

When he got home, Pedro said, "Dad, come see my souvenirs."

His dad smiled, "Why did you choose a shark and a sea turtle?"

"It's a long story," said
Pedro.

"Good," said his dad.
"You can tell me while we
walk Peppy."

Pedro's story was so long, they walked around the block twice.

"Sometimes," said Pedro, "it's fun to go in circles."

And it was!

About the Author

Fran Manushkin is the author
of many popular picture books,
including *Happy in Our Skin*; *Baby,
Come Out!*; *Latkes and Applesauce:
A Hanukkah Story*; *The Tushy
Book*; *Big Girl Panties*; and *Big
Boy Underpants*. Fran writes on
her beloved Mac computer in New York City,
without the help of her two naughty cats,
Chaim and Goldy.

About the Illustrator

Tammie Lyon began her love for
drawing at a young age while
sitting at the kitchen table with
her dad. She continued her love
of art and eventually attended
the Columbus College of Art
and Design, where she earned
a bachelor's degree in fine art. After a brief
career as a professional ballet dancer, she decided
to devote herself full-time to illustration. Today she
lives with her husband, Lee, in Cincinnati, Ohio.
Her dogs, Gus and Dudley, keep her company as she
works in her studio.

Glossary

aquarium (uh-KWAIR-ee-uhm)—a place where collections of water animals and plants are kept and shown

minnows (MIN-ohz)—tiny freshwater fish

snorkel (SNOR-kuhl)—a tube that you use to breathe through when you are swimming under water

souvenir (soo-vuh-NIIIR)—an object that you keep to remind you of a place, a person, or an event

success (suhk-SESS)—a good outcome

Let's Talk

1. How could Pedro have avoided getting separated from his class?

2. How do you think Pedro felt when he realized he was lost?

3. Pretend you are Pedro and explain why you chose shark and sea turtle magnets for souvenirs.

Let's Write

1. List all the sea animals listed in this book. Then draw a picture of your favorite one, and write a sentence about why it is your favorite.

2. Write a story about going on a field trip. It can be either a nonfiction, or true, story or a fiction, or made-up, story.

3. Write down three facts about sharks. If you can't think of three, ask a grown-up to help you find some in a book or on the computer.

JOKE AROUND

⭐ What is a shark's
favorite candy?
jaw breakers

⭐ What do fish take to stay healthy?
vitamin sea

⭐ Who granted the fish's wish?
her fairy cod mother

⭐ Why did the shark cross the road?
to get to the other tide

⭐ How do oysters call
their friends?
on shell phones

⭐ Where do fish keep their money?
in the river bank

⭐ Why won't the shrimp share its toys?
Because it's shellfish.

⭐ What day do fish hate?
Fry-day

⭐ What's the most musical part of a fish?
the scales

⭐ What's the most famous fish in the ocean?
the starfish

RIVER BANK
DEPOSITS